MiND OVER BASKETBALL

YOURSELF TO HANDLE STRESS

D1169823

written by Jane Weierbach, Ph.D.,
and Elizabeth Phillips-Hershey, Ph.D.

illustrated by Charles Beyl

MAGINATION PRESS · WASHINGTON, DC

To Sam, who always plays tight D — *JW*
To Bob, who pays attention to what's happening around him — *EPH*
To all of my fellow gym rats who know the joy of making a good assist — *CB*

Published by
MAGINATION PRESS
An Educational Publishing Foundation Book
American Psychological Association
750 First Street, NE
Washington, DC 20002

For more information about our books, including a complete catalog,
please write to us, call 1-800-374-2721, or visit our website at www.maginationpress.com.

Editor: Darcie Conner Johnston
Art Director: Susan K. White
Project Coordinator: Becky Shaw
Printed by Worzalla, Stevens Point, Wisconsin

Library of Congress Cataloging-in-Publication Data

Weierbach, Jane.
Mind over basketball : coach yourself to handle stress / written by Jane Weierbach, and Elizabeth Phillips-Hershey ; illustrated by Charles Beyl.
        p.   cm.
Summary : Tuck learns to overcome his stress when basketball coach Walton teaches him stress-management and life skills. Includes extensive interactive study guides.
ISBN-13: 978-1-4338-0135-8 (hardcover : alk. paper)
ISBN-10: 1-4338-0135-3 (hardcover : alk. paper)
ISBN-13: 978-1-4338-0136-5 (pbk. : alk. paper)
ISBN-10: 1-4338-0136-1 (pbk. : alk. paper)
1. Youth—Life skills guides—Juvenile literature.   2. Stress in adolescence—Juvenile literature.   3. Basketball—Juvenile literature.   I. Phillips-Hershey, Elizabeth.   II. Beyl, Charles, ill.   III. Title.
HQ796.W365 2007
155.4'18—dc22   2007021351

Manufactured in the United States of America
10 9 8 7 6 5 4 3 2 1

TABLE OF CONTENTS

DEAR READER:

This story is about basketball and kids. It's not a "how to play" book, but a "how to handle the pressures" book. The pressures are the ones we all face, on or off the court. What are the pressures in your life? Maybe you're trying to make the team, or you're handling a heavy load of schoolwork. Maybe you're adjusting to important family changes or dealing with kids who act mean. Whatever the challenges, it may help to know you're not alone.

In *Mind Over Basketball*, Tuck is a kid who deals with similar frustrations. His parents are divorced, and he's had to move to a new town. Tuck lives to play basketball, but he's challenged by a bully who tries to keep him off the court and he can't practice for travel team tryouts. He feels hopeless about making the team, until he realizes that his new coach, Walton, has a few things to teach him.

Walton coaches Tuck about how to handle the stresses that have developed in his life. Stress feels like a big, messy ball of stuff inside you. That stuff might be a combination of worries, hurts, anger, and memories of crummy things that have happened. We all feel stress sometimes. When there is too much stress in our lives, our bodies or our minds (usually both) try to let us know. We may get headaches or stomach pains. We might feel tired all the time, or not be able to fall asleep at night. We might feel nervous or overwhelmed. We might have a short fuse and feel angry or frustrated more than we normally would. We might forget important things.

We can never erase all stress, but we can shrink it to a healthier level. With Walton's help, Tuck learns several strategies that help him keep his cool, make choices that work for him, and focus on the things that deserve attention. Walton also teaches him how to keep his perspective so that little things don't become a bigger deal than they need to be. These are all skills that lower stress. They help us feel calmer, more confident, and more in control of ourselves. And they come in handy no matter what the stress is, no matter what court you're on.

Whether you are reading this book in a group, or with a parent, counselor, or coach, or on your own, you can learn Tuck's stress-busting strategies and use them in your own life. We invite you to **COACH YOURSELF TO HANDLE STRESS** by customizing and practicing the tools in the Coaching Guides between each chapter and by doing the On Your Own exercises at the end of the book. Just like in basketball, a good game plan and practice make the difference when the game begins.

You can do it!

Peace to you,

Jane Weierbach and
Elizabeth Phillips-Hershey

CHAPTER 1

CAN THINGS GET ANY WORSE?

Tuck stepped on to the macadam court at 4th Street and Market. Cars whizzed by. He blew on his fingers and rubbed his hands together. Man, it was cold. At least no one was here. He needed the practice. It felt good to have the basketball back in his hands. He dribbled the ball a couple of times and shot. It hit the backboard and flipped to the side. He caught it on the bounce and shot again. Miss.

"Hey, Jones, check out the new kid!"

Tuck turned. Two boys about a head taller than Tuck stood at the edge of the court.

"Whatcha doin' here, loser?" the one in the red jacket asked. "Think you're gonna play? No way. Not in my house." He bounced his basketball a couple of times.

Tuck turned back to the net and took a shot. WHACK! A ball hit him on the arm. It stung.

"Hey, cut it out!" he said to the one who must be Jones. "It's a free country. I can play here."

The other kid slammed another ball at him. WHACK! "Hey, great!" the kid shouted. "A dodgeball game!"

Jones made a running lunge at Tuck and knocked him flat. He leaned over him with his fist in Tuck's face. "We said *outta here*. You can't even shoot!"

Tuck crab-crawled backward and sprang to his feet. Grabbing his basketball, he ran off, trying to hide the tears. He heard them snickering.

He hated this place.

He missed his home, his friends, his dad, and even his mom, who now worked long hours. He'd never be able to make the basketball travel team.

Life had been terrible since his parents split up: new town, new school, and this dump they called home. His dad lived so far way. No more shooting hoops out by the garage with him. SWISH, SWISH...his dad would tell stories about the Lincoln Nuggets, his high school team. SWISH, SWISH...he loved the story about their championship game. Dad had played forward. That's the position Tuck wanted to play, too.

Tuck hugged the ball to his chest. His heart pounded against it as he ran home. He didn't see the old man until he almost knocked him over. "Outta my way," he sobbed and kept running.

The old man watched him run up to the door of his row house. In the man's hands was a basketball.

Once inside, Tuck threw his jacket on the floor.

"My life stinks!" he fumed. "It's nothing but one big air ball." He kicked the door shut. "Some vacation!"

WHAT IS STRESS?

Are loose basketballs bouncing around in your head? Do you feel like life is one big air ball? Do you wonder whether you can deal with one more thing? Maybe life just keeps sending you another disappointment, failure, or pressure to handle. At least that's the way it feels.

We all feel stressed sometimes—sometimes a lot, sometimes a little. Stress is part of life, especially when something changes that you didn't expect. It also happens when you feel like you can't control what's happening to you.

Stress means that there is a big, messy ball of stuff inside you. That stuff might be a combination of worries, hurts, anger, or memories of crummy things that have happened. We can never erase all stress, but we can shrink stress to a healthier level.

When you're stressed out, your body has several ways of letting you know so that you can do something about it. Do you recognize any of these body stress signals?

- Headache
- Stomachache, no appetite, or overeating
- Tight muscles in your shoulders, neck, or jaw
- Trouble falling asleep or staying asleep

Your mind also has ways of telling you that you're stressed. Do you recognize any of these signals?

- Difficulty focusing on schoolwork, sports, or music lessons

- Forgetting directions or information that people have given you
- Worries about what has already happened or could happen in the future
- Being mad at yourself or criticizing yourself
- "Stuck" thoughts that you can't get out of your head
- "Cluttered" thoughts about all the stuff you have to do
- Feeling tense and nervous
- Feeling frustrated much of the time
- Feeling overwhelmed

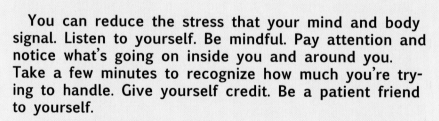

If you have many of the body or mind stress signals in this list, you may be experiencing a large amount of stress. Sometimes you're not aware of how complicated your life is. Sometimes you don't notice the signals that your mind and body are giving you.

You can reduce the stress that your mind and body signal. Listen to yourself. Be mindful. Pay attention and notice what's going on inside you and around you. Take a few minutes to recognize how much you're trying to handle. Give yourself credit. Be a patient friend to yourself.

In the chapters that follow, Walton teaches Tuck several stress-busting strategies that you too can learn once you begin to notice what your body and mind are telling you. These skills will help you relax, feel more confident and in control, and make decisions with good results. They will help you handle stress in every part of your life, no matter what court you're playing on.

TAKE A BASKETBALL BREATH

"**H**oney, this is Walton," said Tuck's mom. "He's a friend of your grandpa's. They used to work together. I invited him to dinner."

Tuck stared across the dinner table at the old man he'd almost knocked down.

"Fried chicken's delicious!" Walton said, pointing a drumstick at Tuck. "So you're a basketball player?"

"Was," Tuck mumbled as he scooped up a spoonful of mashed potatoes.

"Basketball's a great sport. My coaches used to say that it's eighty percent mental and only twenty percent physical."

"Yeah, whatever," Tuck said.

Tuck turned to his mom. "Any chance we can go to the movies tomorrow night?"

"Maybe. Check what's playing and we'll talk about it tomorrow."

"Okay, I'll look." Tuck stood and picked up his dishes. "May I be excused? I think I'll skip the chocolate cake."

His mom sighed. "Sure, Tuck. Walton and I are going to visit for a while. I'll say good night to you before I go to bed."

Tuck glanced at Walton. "See ya."

Walton waved. "Good night, Tuck."

The next morning Tuck had just finished eating his cereal when he heard a knock at the front door.

He checked the peephole and groaned. It was Walton!

"Want to shoot some hoops over at my place?"

"I don't know." Tuck wanted to refuse, but his mom would have a fit. This old guy really thought he could play basketball? As Walton waited for a reply, he twirled the basketball on the tip of a finger. The ball spun for the longest time.

"Won't hurt to give it a try," Walton said. Tuck shrugged his shoulders and retrieved his jacket and ball.

Tuck walked a couple of paces behind as Walton limped ahead. He wore high tops. At least the old man knew good shoes.

I just hope Jones and his friend don't see me, Tuck thought.

Walton's basketball hoop was nailed to the back of his house. He'd shoveled the snow away so there was room to shoot. Tuck dribbled and shot. Air ball. Next time he took careful aim. SWISH. He breathed a sigh of relief. He turned to see if Walton was looking.

Walton smiled. "Nice shot."

Suddenly Walton dribbled the ball, spun, and lifted his arms into the air, his feet barely touching the ground. The ball left his hands in a perfect arc and then hung in the air. SWISH. Two points for the old man.

"Luck," Tuck said to himself and tried to shoot again. Walton danced magic around him. When he was shooting, there was no limp, only smooth, graceful moves. Tuck realized that Walton must have spent years on a court.

Finally Tuck couldn't contain himself any longer. "How do you do it?"

"I breathe."

Tuck snorted. "I breathe, too. No, I mean how do you shoot like that?"

"Seriously, I breathe."

Walton and Tuck shot around a while longer.

"Watch my chest, Tuck. Watch my basketball breath." Walton opened his jacket. As he breathed in, his chest expanded. When he breathed out, his chest went back to normal size. "I call this a basketball breath. Try it."

Tuck laughed. "You gotta be kidding."

"I'm not. Try it a couple of times."

Tuck looked around. He didn't want anyone to see him doing this. He'd be laughed out of his new school before he'd even walked in the front door. He took a big breath in and allowed his chest to expand, then he breathed out. In and out, in and out.

"Here's how I breathe my way through a shot," Walton added. "I breathe in as I'm picking up the basketball and lining it up, and I exhale slowly as I shoot the ball. My eyes are always on the basket. I picture the ball dropping through it, not even touching the rim. Try it."

After a while Walton said, "I'm going inside. I'm cold. Feel free to stay and shoot." He stomped his feet. "Practice it in your head tonight, too. Picture the ball going through the net as you breathe, over and over again."

He limped to his backdoor steps and then looked over his shoulder at Tuck. "If you keep practicing it in your head, you'll be a great shot."

"Hey, Walton...um, thanks." Tuck looked at his ball, then back at Walton. "Any chance you'd help me deal with Jones and that other kid? I really need some court time."

"Tuck, that's for you to handle. Since Jones's dad left, he's been hanging with some rough kids. But come back tomorrow, and I'll give you a few tips."

BECOME YOUR OWN COACH

What makes a good coach?

- A coach notices what works and what doesn't.
- A coach encourages players to learn new skills.
- A coach breaks challenges into small steps.
- A coach insists on practice.
- A coach encourages players to do things for themselves—to be their own coach.

As Walton coaches Tuck to breathe his way into a basketball shot, he is all these things. And as Tuck replays Walton's guidance in his head, he gradually learns to coach himself.

You can be your own coach, too. Whether you're aiming for a spot on the team, a good grade, or breaking an old habit, coaching yourself means you slow down, consider choices, and make a good decision. You notice what works, and you're willing to try new things. When the job looks too big or too hard, you break it down into smaller steps and focus on them one at a time. You keep at it. And you'll get there.

You can even coach yourself to handle stress. Notice the signals in your mind and body, learn the techniques that Walton teaches Tuck for relaxing and centering his mind, and practice them—beginning with the basketball breath and visualization.

The Power of the Breath

The breath is one of the most powerful tools we have for reducing tension and stress in both the mind and the body. It works in three ways:

- The breath brings oxygen into the brain and helps the brain focus, pay attention, and think more clearly.
- The breath brings oxygen to the body and helps the muscles relax.
- The breath slows the heart beat and creates calm.

Walton teaches Tuck a type of breath he calls the basketball breath. The basketball breath is a deep breath that helps you relax and focus your mind, no matter what you're working on.

Follow these steps to relax and focus with the basketball breath:

THE BASKETBALL BREATH

- Place your hand above your waist.
- Slowly take a full breath in through your nose.
- Focus your mind on your breath. Clear your mind of other thoughts as you imagine the air going all the way down to your belly and filling your chest from the bottom up.
- Feel your chest expand.
- Breathe out slowly. Notice that your hand moves as your breath moves.
- Return to your regular breath.

Visualization: The Power of Imagination

Are you trying to learn a skill or do something new, or are you feeling nervous about an upcoming event? Some kids find it helpful to imagine an action or behavior before they try to do it. This is called visualization. Walton teaches this skill to Tuck to help him focus on his foul shot.

Visualizing means that you picture the steps of a new task in your head, sometimes over and over. It's a form of practice that allows you to work out the details of a task in your mind before you actually do it. As you grow more familiar with the task in your mind, you become more skillful and confident. And that means less stress.

Follow these steps to visualize your task or goal:

- Close your eyes. Tune in to your breath. Feel your breath going in and out.
- Pretend you're watching a video of yourself tackling a challenging task exactly the way you want to do it. Picture yourself doing the beginning, middle, and end of the task, one step at a time.
- Ask yourself: What are the details of this picture? What do I like about this picture? What am I doing well? What am I saying to coach myself? What parts of this picture should I change to ace it?
- Rewind the video. Make the necessary changes so that you successfully complete the task exactly the way you really want to do it.
- Practice in your mind. Repeat the visualization, as often as you need to, until you feel confident and ready for the task.

KEEP YOUR COOL

Tuck awakened to eight inches of new snow the next morning. Winter break was almost over. In a couple of days, he'd start his new school.

I'll never make the travel team, he thought. He stared at the snow outside and plopped himself in front of the television. What was the point of going over to that crazy Walton's house anyway? Life stank.

He was halfway through his favorite cartoon when the doorbell rang. There was Walton, with white whiskers and eyebrows, looking like a giant snowman. Two snow shovels leaned against the porch railing. "We need to clear under my basketball net. Then we're off to shovel Mrs. Lafferty's sidewalk."

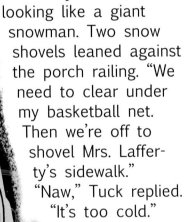

"Naw," Tuck replied. "It's too cold."

"This will help you become a player. Trust me."

Tuck's mouth dropped. This guy was whack.

"You have nothing to lose, Tuck," Walton added. "Get your boots and coat."

All Tuck saw the next couple of hours was flying snow. "How's this going to help my shot?" he grumbled to the snow as Walton moved to clear off someone else's sidewalk.

But he kept shoveling. SPLAT! A big, wet glob of snow fell off a tree limb and landed on his head. He felt it drip down his shirt. *Could things get any worse?* He stabbed the snow with his shovel as he heard Mrs. Lafferty walk out on her front porch. He looked up.

She stood with her hands on her hips. "You're making a mess!" she shouted. "Dig out my mailbox, young man. I can't reach it!"

Tuck threw down his shovel. He stomped down the sidewalk. "Do it yourself!"

Walton waved from the walk next door. "Hello, Mrs. Lafferty," he called. "I think we can manage."

She waved back and went inside.

"How could you be nice to her?" Tuck shouted at Walton. "I'm not dealing with this! I'm outta here!"

"Mrs. Lafferty is an old woman," Walton cautioned. "It must be difficult for her to depend on others. Losing your temper is not going to help." He took Tuck's shovel. "It's just like on the basketball court: Keep your cool. Breathe like I taught you yesterday."

He led Tuck to Mrs. Lafferty's porch steps and motioned Tuck to sit next to him. "Take some nice long breaths right now."

Tuck drew some long breaths. He did feel a little better, but he was still mad. She had a lot of nerve! He breathed some more.

"Listen, Tuck," Walton said after a while. "When you get upset, stop and take a slow breath. Your first reaction is not always the best."

"You mean like yesterday, when I ran away from Jones and his buddy?"

"Maybe that time was okay. But you never know until you take a minute. Any other ideas?"

Tuck shuffled his feet. They felt cold, and he was tired. He didn't feel like a lecture.

"Shovel out her stinkin' mailbox," he mumbled.

"Perhaps, or you could have come for me," Walton added, shifting the shovels off his lap. "You had several choices. Close your eyes now. Picture yourself keeping your cool, just like you pictured the basketball swishing through the net."

Tuck tried to imagine taking a couple of breaths before answering Mrs. Lafferty. It was hard.

"If you can see it," Walton said after a couple of minutes, "you can do it. Come on, we've worked hard enough today. Let's shoot some baskets. Tomorrow we have to chop wood for Mr. Houser."

"Chop wood?" Tuck groaned. But he got in line with Walton, trailing his shovel behind him.

CHOOSE YOUR BEHAVIOR

Everyone can forget that behavior is usually a choice. They react with old stress habits that don't work: they blow up, clam up, or give up. Or sometimes they pretend that the problem isn't happening at all. Can you relate to any of these reactions?

Most of the time kids regret these reactions, because they end up feeling out of control or helpless, or they don't like what happens next. They might lose a friend, make the situation worse, get in trouble with a teacher or parent, or say something they wish could be taken back.

Keeping your cool at challenging times can be difficult. But you can coach yourself to do just that. Taking charge of yourself is taking charge of your behavior. You feel more powerful when you slow down and make thoughtful decisions—when you think before you act.

On the basketball court, the pivot is the move that gives you the time you need to make a thoughtful choice. Without going anywhere, you keep one foot planted on the court and rotate your body around to see your options. You can pass the ball to a teammate, you can dribble to a better shooting position, or you can take the shot.

In life—at school, during a game, with family and friends—think "pivot" to keep your cool. Say to yourself, "I'm going to slow down, breathe, and check out all my choices. Then I'll decide which choice will give me a good result."

As you consider each of your behavior choices, ask yourself, "If I do this, what might happen next?" For example, if you blow up, what might happen? Will this help or hurt you? Or if you decide to talk about the problem later, what might happen? Will this choice help or hurt you? When you give yourself time to think, you're able to recognize the better choices.

A good choice might be to take a break and remove yourself from the situation, or to talk the problem over with a friend or adult you trust. Then, when you take action, you can move forward with confidence.

So remember, here's how you keep your cool with the pivot:

- Stop. Slow yourself down.
- Breathe. Take one full breath.
- Think. Consider your behavior choices and the consequences of each.
- Choose. Decide which behavior choice is best for now, and make a game plan.
- Act. Feel strong by acting on your choice. Stick with your game plan.

THE
PIVOT

TUNE YOUR MIND LiKE A RADio

Tuck's days were filled with chopping wood, shoveling snow, practicing basketball at Walton's house—and worrying. How would he ever make the travel team? He wasn't getting court time. When school started, Tuck was still practicing at Walton's.

Walton was a good coach. He broke the various basketball skills into small steps. One afternoon they practiced reverse layups. "Think tall, think sky!" Walton shouted. "You've got to coach yourself!"

Another afternoon it was the spin move. With chopping wood and shoveling, Tuck felt stronger as he hustled around Walton.

"You know the change-up pitch in baseball?" Walton called out. "That's the pitch they don't expect." Tuck nodded. "Well, basketball is the same. Cut and change direction. That's right! You're getting quicker on your feet."

Tuck and Walton took turns shooting fouls.

"Did you ever play on a team, Walton?"

Walton nodded. "I was on the varsity hoops team at Stanford until my car accident."

"The limp?"

"Yes, I'm lucky to be alive." Walton looked down at his leg. "Lost my chance to play college and pro ball. The accident was not my fault. I felt bitter and angry for a long time."

Tuck plopped down on the snow bank, breathing heavily. "Me too. If my parents hadn't divorced, I'd be on the travel team at my old school. Now I'll never have that chance." He shook his head. "I can't even get court time."

Walton sat down next to him. "Tuck," Walton said, "It's best not to go there. You'll never get anywhere if you think that way."

Tuck shrugged.

"You've got to change the way you think. I had to. Replaying angry thoughts about the past—I call them shoulda, coulda, woulda thoughts—couldn't change what happened to me. The only thing it did was make me miserable. All the time."

Walton shook his head. "I finally got sick of it, and decided I felt better when I wasn't so negative. I thought, I know how to play basketball. Maybe I can teach others. That's why I coach kids to play basketball now. I changed my angry thoughts to something more positive. And I'm happier."

Tuck opened his mouth to speak, but before he could get a word out, Walton placed his hand on Tuck's shoulder. "I know. I know. Worries pop into your mind like loose basketballs." Walton stood up and tossed his basketball from hand to hand.

"You know the scanner on a radio," he continued, "how it flips from one station to another? You can tune your mind just like you choose the music you like. That's what I did when I started coaching basketball. I found a new way to think about basketball. I changed my station."

Walton tossed the basketball to Tuck. "Think about the basketball moves you know instead of all this 'I can't' stuff. Think about your game plan. Choose the positive station."

He turned and called to Tuck, "Let's go. I want you to practice boxing out on defense. Tomorrow you're ready to take on Jones, one on one. Tomorrow, you keep your cool."

TALK POSITIVELY TO YOURSELF

Do you hear yourself saying "I can't"? Maybe you think you're not good enough to make the team. Or you won't be able to learn your lines for the school play. Or kids don't like you. Or you're no good at spelling. You think, "If I were taller...stronger...smarter, then I could...." Or like Tuck, you think, "If that hadn't happened, everything would be fine."

These are nega-tive thoughts. Some of them can be called shoulda, coulda, woulda thoughts. They don't help you. In fact, they can hurt you by stressing you out, making you feel bad about yourself, and distracting you from doing your best.

You don't choose which thoughts or worries pop into your head. But you can limit how long your mind stays stuck on them. You can think of your mind as a radio, and tune it to a different station—a station without the static of negative thoughts that just bring you down. Choose a positive station instead. Choose to think thoughts that help you keep your perspective.

Keeping your perspective means that you focus on the facts—things you've done and things you know—to remind yourself that your goal is a realistic one.

Here are some examples:

- I have practiced a lot. I have a good chance to make the team.
- It may take a while, but I will learn long division.
- I know how to make friends. I've done it many times. I will ask John to play ball at recess.
- I have done this before, so I know I can do it again.
- My writing improved a lot last year. I can use those better writing skills this year.

By keeping your perspective, you're tuned to what is real and true, instead of feeling overwhelmed or worrying about shoulda, coulda, woulda. When you tune to a positive station, you can coach yourself to feel in control and to do your genuine best.

BRiNG YouR A-gAME

The sun peeked into Tuck's window, awakening him. Saturday. He glanced at the clock and yawned. Plenty of time. Under his covers, he felt warm and relaxed. But thoughts of the morning ahead gradually intruded on his peacefulness. What if Jones overpowered him again? What if he couldn't make a shot? His chest tightened. His palms started to sweat. Not this again!

Then Tuck heard Walton's words: "Think about how you're going to play your game, instead of thinking all this 'I can't' stuff."

He took a basketball breath. Already he felt his head start to clear. No matter what he was doing on the court, he wanted to use his full breath. He reminded himself that defense was the bottom line for any game. He pictured himself playing tight D by staying close to his man. He grew tall on his rebounds and snagged them. As he breathed deeply, he felt more solid, more confident, more relaxed.

The smell of French toast reminded Tuck that there was more to life than basketball. Man, he was hungry! But he'd better get moving if he was going to have time to warm up before Jones showed up at the court.

"Big morning?" Mom asked, watching him eat.

He nodded. He wasn't sure there was a lot to say—just now anyway. After the scrimmage with Jones, he'd share what he'd learned. His mom knew what was up. But right now he couldn't talk.

Tuck got up, placed his dishes on the counter, and grabbed his basketball. His mom met him at the door with his coat. She gave him a high-five and a hug.

The court was empty. Tuck warmed up with easy jumpers. He found himself breathing along with his shots and watching the ball as it dropped through the net. SWISH! Another SWISH! He felt free and easy for the first time in a long time. Maybe there really was something to this breath thing of Walton's.

Out of the corner of his eye he saw a tall kid walk toward the court, bouncing a basketball. Jones. Party's over, thought Tuck. He's gonna be all over me in a second.

Tuck caught himself holding his breath and realized he was tuned to a negative station.

"Change the channel," he said to himself. "Tune to the positive station." He coached himself with more of Walton's words: Just breathe. Remember the facts. I'm strong and I've been practicing.

"Hey, loser, 'ssup?" Jones called out as he heaved the ball at Tuck. This time instead of ducking, Tuck caught it, dribbled, took a breath, and shot. SWISH! Nothing but net. Jones caught the ball before it hit the ground, took it out to half court, and began to drive toward the basket.

Tuck thought: Defense. Breathe.

He stayed between Jones and the basket, even in the air on Jones's layup. The ball hit the rim, looked like it would drop in, but bounced out. Tuck hustled for the rebound. He had wings on his sneakers. Both boys grabbed for the ball, but Tuck got there first. Jones gave him an elbow. Tuck tuned it out and dribbled to half court.

Fast break: Tuck drove to the basket with Jones stuck to him like glue. Tuck led with his shoulder as he cut his own path to the hole. Tuck's heart was beating like a drum. He pump faked, Jones bought it, Tuck rose again. With a breath, Tuck lofted the ball in the air. It found the net.

"Not bad, for a loser," muttered Jones as he dribbled the ball to half court. Tuck held his smile inside. Jones took a long jumper, got plenty of height, followed through perfectly, and whistled as the ball dropped through the net. Jones had an excellent shot, but he really could use some work on his attitude.

They traded possessions for the next hour. Even in the January snow, both boys were sweating as they covered the court, again and again, breathing as fast as their feet were racing. Tuck wasn't keeping score, but he guessed it was about even up.

"Gotta go, man," said Jones. "My mom has chores for me. Gotta get them done before I go to my dad's. This divorce, two houses thing is really a drag. Hey, we usually play a pickup game here on Sunday afternoons.

Maybe we'll let you play tomorrow." He took one last shot. SWISH. "Looks like you and I would have home court advantage," he added with a smirk.

"Sounds good. I'll be there," Tuck said, as casually as possible.

Tuck stayed on the court and shot a few more after Jones left. He was walking on air.

I held my own. I didn't fold. I kept my cool. I played my own game.

He heard the familiar sound of Walton's basketball shuffle. "I checked you out," Walton said. "You brought your A-game."

"Yeah," Tuck grinned, "I was swishing threes like crazy. Jones was, too. He's a real player!"

"You too, Tuck," Walton said. "And you've picked up a few new moves."

"I breathed."

"You looked like you were tuned to right now."

"If I can go head to head with Jones, the travel team is a done deal."

"Not so fast," Walton said as he dribbled. "Better stay tuned to right now. You never know when I might stuff you while you're counting your chickens."

Walton blew by Tuck, drifted into the air and laid the ball gracefully in the hoop like it was a basket of Easter eggs. "Better keep your mind on now. If you keep your cool now, the future will take care of itself."

FOCUS ON NOW

Do you worry about the future? Like Tuck, are you stressed about something that's coming up? A worry is a thought that looks ahead to something that may or may not go wrong. It is what-ifing. You think, "What if I fail the test?" or "What if I don't make the team?"

Your mind may want to skip ahead, thinking about the future instead of what's happening right now. That's natural, but it can be confusing and overwhelming. It can turn into a worry that gets in the way of what you need to do or that distracts you from enjoying the moment.

There's a difference between worrying about something in the future and making a plan for it. Take that math test, for example. Worrying "What if I fail?" is not going to change the outcome. It doesn't help in any way. It only stresses you out. What does help is making a behavior choice and an action plan. Instead of what-ifing about the test, you can remind yourself: "I have made a study plan. I know I'll be ready for the test. I can relax." Then you can focus on now.

Use the power of your mind to turn off worries and pay attention to the activity that you're doing this moment. Be mindful.

Here are some ways you can focus on now:

If you're what-ifing about something in the future, pull your mind out of the future and focus on the present. Notice your thoughts and narrow them down to what's happening right now. For example, think,

- "I can listen to the teacher's directions instead of thinking about a test I'm not even taking yet and wondering how hard it will be."
- "I can watch the game and notice what the players are doing instead of worrying about whether I will make the shot when I get on the court."

If you're feeling overwhelmed by a big project and thinking you can't do all of it, break the task into steps and figure out one small thing you can do now. For example, think,

- "I can focus on learning just the right-hand part of this song I'm playing on the piano."
- "I can focus on keeping my foot planted while I pivot."

If you're worried about something that needs to be done, turn your full attention to it and take action now. Do something about it, then move on. For example, think,

- "I'm going to put my notebook in my backpack now so I don't forget to take it to school tomorrow."
- "I'm feeling unsure about my reverse layup. I'm going to practice for half an hour now."
- "I'm worried about that book report due next week. Right now I will make a study plan and read the first three chapters."
- "I'm scared I will forget my lines. I'm going to visualize my scene in the play and go over the lines in my head."
- "I am making a list of the things I need to do in the morning, so I can relax and go to sleep."

If your mind is cluttered with thoughts but it's not the right time for action, focus on a simple distraction in the here and now. For example, if you're trying to fall asleep, think,

- "I can focus on the rhythm of my breath."
- "I can pay attention to how warm my feet are under the covers."
- "I can look at the way the street light makes shadows on my wall."

What-if worrying is a waste of your time and energy. It's a big source of stress. Reduce your what-if stress by practicing these techniques for pulling your mind out of the future and into the now.

CHAPTER 6

STiCK To yoUR gAME PLAN

Two weeks later...

The first day of the tryouts finally arrived. Tuck walked down 4th Street. Loose basketballs bounced in his head. His stomach was in knots.

"What if I don't make the team?" he worried.

Walton's words came to mind. Tuck changed the station. He took a deep breath. "I'm prepared," he said to himself, and walked into the gym.

There wasn't a gymnasium he didn't love, this one included. There was something about the sound of basketballs bouncing on the floor and voices ricocheting off the walls that made him hungry—hungry for a good game. Oh, he wanted to make this team!

"Who's in charge?" he asked another kid standing at the entrance. The kid just shrugged his shoulders and walked away. Tuck looked around. Over in the corner was a woman with a clipboard. He walked in her direction.

After signing the roster, he dropped his jacket on the bleachers and moved onto the floor. He took a shot from the right corner. SWISH! That felt good. He hustled to retrieve the ball, but a big kid rushed in at the same time, elbowing Tuck in the shoulders. Whoa, Tuck thought, this guy is tall. He glanced at another kid who was driving in for a layup. Same height! Am I in the right place? These guys look like they're in high school. What do they feed them anyway?

Tuck started to feel nervous. And he noticed he felt that way. He took a deep breath, then coached himself to keep his perspective: Calm down. I'm okay. Some of these guys are taller than I am, but some are my height, too.

A whistle blew. Everyone formed two lines for the layup drill. Tuck's partner sent him a wild pass. He missed his layup. Second time around, the guy gave him a late pass. Was the kid sending him bad passes on purpose? Tuck tried to catch his eye. But the kid avoided his look. Tuck was bummed. Shake it off and move on, he coached himself. Stay in the now. He needed his complete focus.

The coaches divided the players into teams for a scrimmage. Tuck in-bounded the ball to his teammate, who dribbled down the court and went for a layup without passing. He missed. Tuck thought, ball hog!

The other team got the rebound and moved for the fast break. The tall kid that Tuck guarded drove for the basket, obviously elbowing Tuck out of the way. The whistle blew. Flagrant offensive foul!

Tuck took his place at the foul line. Okay, I got this covered, he thought. Just use the basketball breath and picture the ball sinking through the hoop.

He scored on both free throws. Tuck smiled. His practice was paying off.

Better focus, Tuck thought, as he hustled to half court. Remember, we still have the ball. He glanced at the clock and saw five seconds left in the half. He passed the ball to the point guard, who attempted the buzzer beater. SWOOSH! The three-ball fell. What a way to end the half!

Tuck didn't start the second half. As he stood on the sidelines, he refused to worry about it. He kept his perspective, telling himself that other kids needed game time. As he checked out the action, he noticed there was no traffic on the left side of the other team's basket. So he put the left side of their basket in his game plan. Force them to go to the left, where they're weak.

The coach motioned Tuck on to the court. One of his teammates passed the ball to him. He almost froze but instead used the pivot to check out all his options.

He one-eightied and saw an open teammate. He sent a sweet little bounce pass to him. The guy squared up and shot. That's what I'm talking about! Two points, maybe three!

Tuck's man started to drive toward the basket. Tuck played tough and forced him to the left. His man took a jumper, but he was off balance. The ball bounced off the rim. Tuck bolted for the rebound and grabbed it just before it bounced out of bounds. He managed to flip it to a teammate.

Good game plan, Tuck thought. As he hustled down court, stinging sweat rolled down his face and into his eyes. He was playing tight D. This was fun! Exhaling a

big breath, he reminded himself: Stay focused on now. Watch that ball.

The first day of tryouts was over. One more day to go. Tuck's mind was in a whirl, with so much to sort through. It wasn't all good or all bad. He needed to talk to Walton.

Tuck found Walton at home with his leg propped on a pillow.

"I tried to think positive, but man, it was hard!" Tuck looked down at Walton. He didn't look too good.

"What did you do?" asked Walton.

"The layup drill started out really rough. My partner didn't play fair," Tuck responded. "It was like he was trying to throw me off. But I put the layup drill behind me and stayed in the present moment when we scrimmaged. I focused on what I had to do right then and played tight defense." Tuck paced back and forth. "It helped. I didn't do half bad. Made plenty of assists. Sure hope the coaches saw that I was a team player."

Tuck sat down next to Walton. "You should have seen me at the foul line. I focused, I breathed, I pictured the ball going through the hoop."

"Sounds like you used the power of your mind on and off the court, Tuck. You pictured how you were going to play before you got there. And you stuck to your game plan. You've come a long way since Jones."

Tuck and Walton sat in silence for a couple of minutes. Tuck glanced at Walton. "Any chance we could go outside and shoot some hoops, Walton?"

"Can't. My leg."

"I'm sorry." Tuck looked from Walton's face to his leg. "You're in pain. I shouldn't have asked."

"That's okay. Some days there are more challenges off the court than on the court. This is one of them. But I've found it pays to find something positive about the way things really are, rather than wishing things were different. Besides, I'd rather think about your success on the court today. Tuck, I think you have what it takes to play your A-game tomorrow. Just keep your focus. Stick to your game plan."

The next day, Tuck arrived early at the gym. He thought, today is the day I find out if I make the travel team. Tomorrow is the big math test and the first school dance and.... Whoa, he laughed to himself, stay in the present. You've got enough to handle right now.

He glanced around the gym. One of his teammates from yesterday waved to him. Tuck smiled, breathed, and took his place on the court.

COACH YOURSELF TO HANDLE STRESS

Just like Tuck, your life may have its ups and downs. As you read this story, you may have identified stressful things in your life. You may not be satisfied with how you're dealing with problem situations. But you, too, can learn how to coach yourself to handle stress. Take a deep breath, read, and reflect on the following questions. When you're ready, write your responses. It's time to create your own game plan.

HOW DO YOU KNOW WHEN YOU ARE STRESSED OUT?

What are your body stress signals?

1 _____

2 _____

3 _____

What are your mind stress signals?

1 _____

2 _____

3 _____

WHEN TUCK WANTED TO COACH HIMSELF TO HANDLE STRESS, WHAT DID HE DO?

☐ He took full breaths. He practiced the basketball breath.

☐ He caught himself listening to negative thoughts. He changed his thoughts to the positive station. He limited his shoulda, coulda, woulda thoughts.

☐ He focused on what he could do right now. He blew the whistle on his what-if worries.

☐ He visualized himself making foul shots and rebounds.

☐ He accepted help and coaching from Walton. He gave Walton's suggestions a chance.

☐ _____

_____

☐ _____

_____

WHEN YOU WANT TO COACH YOURSELF TO HANDLE STRESS, WHAT WILL YOU DO?

Who is on Your STRESS-BuSTiNg TEAM?

No one can do it by himself or herself. Accepting help from others is a sign of strength. Where can you get help?

Write the names of kids you can count on. Include kids who have good ideas or are good listeners.

1 _____

2 _____

3 _____

4 _____

5 _____

A teacher, parent or other family member, counselor, therapist, or coach can be part of your team. Which adults could you include on your stress-busting team?

1 _____

2 _____

3 _____

4 _____

5 _____

How Will You Know You're Coaching Yourself To Handle Stress?

☐ You remember you have the power to choose how to behave—what to do and what to say.

BIG TEST NEXT WEEK!

☐ You remember that "what if" is only a stressful thought about the future, and that you can focus instead on what you can do right now.

☐ You break the task into small steps.

STUDY ½ HOUR EVERY DAY

☐ You are patient with yourself. You give yourself time to learn new skills.

☐ You praise yourself after each step.

☐ You remember to keep your perspective. You remind yourself of the facts and what you already know to be true.

LESS STRESS ON TEST DAY

☐ _____
_____

☐ _____
_____

WHAT PERSONAL CHALLENGES DO YOU WANT TO HANDLE BETTER?

1 _____
_____
_____

2 _____
_____
_____

3 _____
_____
_____

WHAT SUGGESTIONS WOULD YOU GIVE YOURSELF AS YOUR OWN PERSONAL COACH?

1 _____
_____
_____

2 _____
_____
_____

3 _____
_____
_____

WHAT WILL YOU NOTICE IS DIFFERENT WHEN YOU COACH YOURSELF IN A POSITVE WAY?

- ☐ You sleep better.

- ☐ Your body has fewer aches.
- ☐ You laugh and smile more often.
- ☐ Frustration is something you're learning to handle.
- ☐ _____
- ☐ _____
  _____
- ☐ _____
  _____

SWISH!

THE BASKETBALL FLOWS THROUGH THE NET. LIKE A GREAT PLAYER, YOU ARE MOVING FREE AND EASY. WINGS ARE ON YOUR SNEAKS. **GO FOR IT!**